Up in Flames

Dare or Danger

by

Sue Graves

Illustrated by Aleksandar Sotirovski

With special thanks to our readers:
Jasper Allden
Jack Bradford-Smith
Aimee Chambers
Lizzie Giddings
Luke Giddings
Rachel Nalletamby
Josh Rose
Ashley Sands
Kendall Sommersett
Harvey Williams

First published in 2010 in Great Britain by
Barrington Stoke Ltd
18 Walker St, Edinburgh, EH3 7LP

www.barringtonstoke.co.uk

ISBN: 978-1-84299-773-4

Printed in Great Britain by The Charlesworth Group

Danger! We ask the author a tricky question ...

Have you ever saved the day?

When I was seven, I came home from school to find the kitchen full of yellow smoke! My dog, Dinah, was barking at the door to be let out. I let her out into the garden and waited with her until my parents came home. They were shocked to see the mess in the kitchen. The whole room was yellow! The smoke had come from our boiler. They quickly phoned for someone to mend it.

For James, Caroline, Giles,
Camilla and Bridget.

Dan and Lee were playing football
behind the old people's homes.

Suddenly the coin Lee had found in the woods fell out of his pocket. Would it say **dare** or **danger**? It hummed and landed **danger** side up.

Dan grinned. "There's no danger here," he said, pointing to the old people's homes. "Old people aren't a danger to anyone!"

But Lee *didn't* grin. He was looking hard at the homes.

"Something's up," he said. "There's some smoke coming from that one."

"I expect it's a bonfire," said Dan.

"No way!" said Lee. "Come on! Let's find out what's going on."

The boys ran to have a closer look.
Smoke was coming out of the open kitchen
window.

They looked in and saw flames coming from a bin.

Worse still, a small dog was jumping up at the door trying to get out.

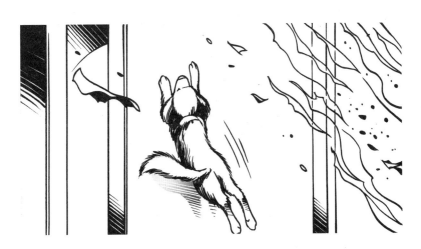

"Call 999 and get the fire service, Lee," said Dan. "I'll get the dog."

He climbed in the window and grabbed
the dog. He handed the dog out of the
window to Lee.

"Get out of there *now*, Dan!" said Lee.

"The fire is only inside the bin," said Dan. "I think I can put it out before it gets worse."

Dan filled a pan with water and threw it into the bin. But the flames were still there.

Then Lee saw a hose. He pushed the hose in the window and turned on the tap. The water shot out of the hose. It knocked over the bin. It knocked over Dan, too.

"You idiot!" yelled Dan. "I'm dripping wet!"

"Yes," grinned Lee. "But the fire is out!"

Just then the fire engine arrived with its
lights flashing.

"It was quick of you to do all that," said one of the fire fighters when she saw what Dan and Lee had done. "Well done!"

Just then the old lady who lived there came home.

"I threw my fag end into the bin. But I forgot to put it out first!" said the old lady. She patted her dog. "Thank you for saving Scruffy."

Then she saw how wet Dan was. She saw how wet her kitchen was, too.

"Sorry about the mess," said Dan.

The old lady smiled. "I think we had better get you and my kitchen dry," she said. "Then I'll make us all some tea!"

Like this book? Why not try the next one?

Doom Ride

The coin lands on its side! **Dare** *and* **Danger**!

Lee and Dan go on a roller coaster. But the ride goes wrong. Can the boys save themselves – and their friend?

For more info check out our website:
www.barringtonstoke.co.uk